P9-BYF-794

Jolly Roger

A DOG OF HOBOKEN

by

Manus

~~Daniel M.~~ Pinkwater

Lothrop, Lee & Shepard Books
New York

The pictures in this book were made using an Apple Macintosh computer, and the MacPaint program. The author drew the pictures with a "mouse," which is a little rolling box connected to the computer by a wire. The pictures appeared on the computer screen in the form of little dots called "pixels." When each picture was finished, it was printed on a dot matrix printer (the sort of printer used with most computers).

First Edition   1 2 3 4 5 6 7 8 9 10

LIBRARY OF CONGRESS CATALOGING IN PUBLICATION DATA

Pinkwater, Daniel Manus, (date)
  Jolly Roger, a dog of Hoboken.

   Summary: Chronicles the adventures of the remarkable canine who became the undisputed king of Hoboken's dockside dogs.
   1. Children's stories, American. [1. Dogs—Fiction] I. Title.
PZ7.P6335Jo 1985   [Fic]   84-12629
ISBN 0-688-03898-0   ISBN 0-688-03899-9 (lib. bdg.)

To the lady who takes care
of Ziggy, Bear, Flake,
and me

THIS IS THE STORY of Jolly Roger, a dockside dog of Hoboken. There are a lot of stories about Jolly Roger—some of them may be true and some may not—but Jolly Roger was a real dog, and lots of people remember him.

I

Jolly Roger came to Hoboken on a ship from Alaska, the *Matilda Magoo*. It was named for the captain's sister. The captain was Matthew Magoo, and he was a good captain too. The only thing wrong with Captain Magoo was that he was too soft-hearted. He would allow little privileges to the men

in his crew, and little favors, and permission to do this and that, and soon things would get out of hand. For example, there was the matter of pets. First a sailor came on board with a little gray kitten. The sailor's name was Norway Ned.

"Oh, please, please, please, Captain Magoo, let me keep the kitten!" Norway Ned had said. Captain Magoo told Norway Ned he could keep the kitten as long as he remembered to feed it and didn't let the kitten make a mess of things aboard ship.

The kitten named Mitten was a great favorite of the sailors, and when the *Matilda Magoo* came into port again, a sailor named Jutland Jed came aboard with a kitten of his own, a black one named Nitten.

"You allowed Norway Ned to have a kitten," Jutland Jed said to Captain Magoo. "I've been on this ship twice as long as Norway Ned, so I should be allowed to have a kitten too."

Of course, there was nothing for Captain Magoo to do except allow Jutland Jed to keep his kitten named Nitten.

At the next port a sailor named Fiji Fred brought five kittens aboard—never mind what their names were. He went to see Captain Magoo.

"I work five times as hard as Norway Ned and Jutland Jed," Fiji Fred said. "So I should be allowed to keep my five kittens, never mind what their names are."

What could Captain Magoo do but say yes?

It wasn't long before the ship became a sort of floating zoo. The crew had kittens and cats, dogs and parrots, rats and mice, monkeys, fish, snakes, and even spiders.

Captain Magoo got fed up. "This is what comes of my being nice to Norway Ned!" he said. "I'm go-

ing to put my foot down! The next port we strike, every animal goes off this ship. I mean it!"

The next port for the *Matilda Magoo* was Hoboken. Captain Magoo told the crew they had forty-eight hours to sell, trade, or give away their animals. The sailors were unhappy about the orders, but a sailor always obeys his captain, so they trooped into town to sell, trade, and give away their pets.

At the end of two days the crew of the *Matilda Magoo* had sold, swapped, and made presents of cats and dogs and mice and parrots and any number of animals—all except a puppy belonging to a sailor named Texas Ted. This puppy was Texas Ted's pride and joy. It was half Chinese Chow Chow, and half Alaskan Husky. Its name was Jolly Roger.

Texas Ted just couldn't find anyone to give his puppy to. The fact is, he didn't want to give his puppy to anyone, and he didn't look very hard. He hoped that somehow Captain Magoo would change his mind and let him keep Jolly Roger. Texas Ted was the oldest and toughest sailor on the *Matilda Magoo*. He didn't really believe that the captain would force him to give up his Chow Chow Husky puppy. When the time came to sail, Captain Magoo gave Texas Ted his orders: "As captain of this vessel, I order you to put that pooch ashore, period."

Texas Ted was rough and tough, but he was a good sailor, and he knew that orders are orders. He carried Jolly Roger down the gangplank, and looked around for someone to give him to. "Tie him to that post," Captain Magoo said, "and let's get underway!"

Texas Ted couldn't do that—but the *Matilda*

Magoo was about to weigh anchor—and Ted knew he must do his duty. Just then, The Kid came along. The Kid was a Hoboken kid. He earned his living parking cars in a parking lot. "Hey, Kid," Texas Ted said. "You want this puppy?"

And that is how Jolly Roger came to Hoboken.

II

The Kid had a job in a parking garage in Hoboken, and that's where he took Jolly Roger. The Kid's boss was called Marvin the Ape.

"Hey Kid, you're twelve minutes late," Marvin the Ape said. "You want I should fire you and maybe jump up and down on your head?"

"Hey, don't hit me Boss!" The Kid said. "Look, I got this puppy!"

"Awww, he's cute," Marvin the Ape said. "What's his name?"

"His name is Jolly Roger, Boss. He came off a ship from Alaska. He's part Chinese Chow Chow, and part Alaskan Husky. His father was the toughest dog in Fairbanks. A sailor gave him to me."

"Well, get to work, or I'll tie knots in your arms and legs—and that would upset the puppy. Kootchie–koo, little Jolly Roger," Marvin the Ape said.

The Kid's job was to wash cars, and wax cars, and park cars for people when they brought them into the garage, and to go and get the cars for those people when they came back. Every day The Kid would take Jolly Roger to work. Every day Marvin the Ape would shout threats at The Kid and secretly give cookies to Jolly Roger.

Jolly Roger had his own doghouse inside the garage, near the place where The Kid washed cars. Washing cars was Jolly Roger's favorite activity at the garage.

In those days Jolly Roger liked everybody, and played with all the people who came to the garage— like any puppy. But Alaskan Huskies in general, and Chinese Chow Chows in particular, are not the sort of dogs to play with just anyone. Alaskan Huskies and Chinese Chow Chows are both very particular breeds. They have their dignity. As Jolly Roger grew up he stopped romping with people—and he did not allow people to pet him.

The only exception was The Kid. The Kid could throw a ball for Jolly Roger to chase, and wrestle with Jolly Roger, and get Jolly Roger to lie on his back and wave all four paws in the air.

It bothered Marvin the Ape. "How come The

Kid is the only person Jolly Roger wants to play with?" he asked. "I have been giving him cookies for a year."

That's the way it sometimes is with Alaskan Huskies and Chinese Chow Chows.

III

Ordinarily, it is not such a good idea to let dogs roam around loose, especially in a busy place like Hoboken—but in Jolly Roger's case there was no choice. The Kid had nothing to say about it. One day Jolly Roger disappeared around the corner and was gone for three hours.

The Kid was worried about Jolly Roger but Marvin the Ape said, "Listen—dogs will be dogs. You've got to let Jolly Roger go around by himself or the other dogs will think he's a weenie."

It was good advice. It was also notable that Marvin the Ape did not threaten The Kid.

When Jolly Roger came back he looked worn out. He also was covered with mud, and he appeared to have been chewed on. He was tired. He was thirsty. He drank a great deal of water. Jolly Roger was obviously very happy. The Kid got the hose, the one he washed cars with, and gave Jolly Roger a bath.

"I guess Jolly Roger found some other dogs to play with," Marvin the Ape said. "By the way, you don't expect to use my water for free, do you?"

After the first time, Jolly Roger went off by himself every day—and he stayed away longer every time. The Kid tried tying Jolly Roger up, but the Chow Chow Husky cried and whined and chewed at the rope until The Kid let him go. Sometimes Jolly Roger would be gone all day.

The Kid began spending his lunch hour wandering around Hoboken looking for Jolly Roger. He found him. Jolly Roger was spending time with the

dock dogs. The dock dogs were the rough, tough
dogs of the Hoboken waterfront. For blocks along
River Street there was a big iron fence. Behind the
fence were docks where ships came to load and un-
load. The area behind the fence belonged to the
rough tough longshoremen who did the loading and
unloading, and to the rough tough dock dogs. Jolly
Roger had made friends with both the longshoremen
and the dogs.

These dogs were three-quarters wild. No one could touch them. They ran and played and fought behind the iron fence. The longshoremen shared their lunches with the dogs and chased away the Hoboken dog catcher whenever he came. At night the wild Hoboken dock dogs ran through the streets of the waterfront neighborhood, knocking over garbage cans, barking, and lunging at cats. These were the dogs that adopted Jolly Roger, the young dog from Alaska.

IV

The leader of the dock dogs was a big black dog. Some of the longshoremen called him Brutus MacDougal Bugleboy. He was some tough dog. Some said Brutus MacDougal Bugleboy was part Labrador Retriever, some said he was part Newfoundland dog. Most people said and believed that he was part African Upland Gorilla.

Brutus MacDougal Bugleboy had a nasty temper. The Hoboken dock dogs knew it. The rough tough longshoremen knew it. More than once a big strong longshoreman, who carried 200 pound bags of coffee beans on his shoulder, had to be rescued from the top of a big crate by other longshoremen because Brutus MacDougal Bugleboy had taken a sudden dislike to him. If Brutus MacDougal Bugleboy liked someone he would just ignore that person.

It was Brutus MacDougal Bugleboy that Jolly Roger had his fight with. It didn't happen right away. At first, when Jolly Roger began hanging out with the wild Hoboken dock dogs, he was little more than a puppy. Jolly Roger was polite to every one of the dock dogs. They, in turn, teased him, and chased him, and took special pleasure in rolling him in the mud until he looked like a giant dirtball, but no dog ever hurt him. Except Brutus MacDougal Bugleboy. Brutus bit Jolly Roger, painfully, right on the nose. Brutus MacDougal Bugleboy did that to every new dog in the pack. It was his favorite trick. It was Brutus MacDougal Bugleboy's intention that the new dog remember the bite, and remember to be afraid of Brutus.

Jolly Roger remembered the bite, but he also

remembered that he had not had a chance to bite Brutus MacDougal Bugleboy on *his* nose. Jolly Roger planned to do that. In fact, Jolly Roger planned to chase Brutus MacDougal Bugleboy away, and become leader of the dock dogs himself— just like that. Some dogs are dominant. (That means they *have* to run things.) Jolly Roger was a dominant dog. Either he would be the boss of the Hoboken dock dogs, or he would leave the docks forever and live off scraps in alleys in the back of town. Jolly Roger did not expect to lose the fight. It would be Brutus MacDougal Bugleboy who would live on handouts in the alley.

And that is exactly what happened. Those who saw the fight said it was not much. Jolly Roger walked up to Brutus MacDougal Bugleboy one day and bit him, very hard, on the nose. There was some scuffling and growling, and Brutus MacDougal Bugleboy took off for the back of town. He was never seen on the waterfront again. Brutus knew that Jolly Roger was the better dog, and he didn't stay around to find out just how much better.

Jolly Roger didn't have a scratch on him. He looked around, offering to fight any other dog that was interested. No dogs were interested. Then the wild Hoboken dog pack settled back into its normal routine, with one exception: Jolly Roger was king of the waterfront.

V

Jolly Roger started staying out all night. Sometimes The Kid would not see his dog for two or three days. Jolly Roger was an important citizen. As king of the waterfront, Jolly Roger had many things to do. First of all, he had to receive the respects of all the other dogs. There were the regular dock dogs,

strangers passing through, and house pets who would run away and join the dock dogs for a day and then go home. Some dogs were let out each morning by their owners to spend the day on the waterfront, and at night they would go home. One man drove in each day from another town with two pedigreed hunting dogs. The hunting dogs would spend the day on the docks while their master worked, and go home with him at night.

All these dogs had to go and see Jolly Roger every day. Jolly Roger would lie in the patch of grass behind the big iron fence in the morning, and each dog would slink up to him with its head held sideways, and put its muzzle under Jolly Roger's chin,

or sniff his whiskers. This is a way dogs have of showing respect. Jolly Roger would give a little sniff to each dog to let it know he had accepted its greeting. Sometimes there would be twenty or thirty dogs taking part in this ceremony.

Jolly Roger decided which dogs would be allowed to stay with the pack, and which would be chased away. He broke up fights, and protected young and small dogs. He never bit any dog on the nose as Brutus had done—and he got into very few fights. Most dogs decided from the look of Jolly Roger that they didn't want to fight with him.

Jolly Roger got first sniff at any food the longshoremen offered the dock dogs. If Jolly Roger didn't like the smell of it, and didn't eat any, neither did the other dogs.

Jolly Roger decided who the pack should be afraid of and who they should and should not like. Many of the dock dogs had never been touched by a human, and they were afraid of them. Jolly Roger was comfortable with people and understood them—so the dock dogs depended on his judgment of the humans they met.

Jolly Roger protected mother dogs and new puppies. The puppies all looked like him. He picked

out safe, secret places for the puppies to be hidden, and helped to guard them.

When the weather began to grow cold, Jolly Roger would show the younger dogs how to sweep newspaper and leaves together under parked cars and against walls to make warm nests to sleep in.

The most important thing Jolly Roger did was to teach the other dogs how to keep away from the Hoboken municipal dog catcher. The dog catcher drove around in a little truck. His dearest wish was to catch every one of the Hoboken dock dogs. One trick Jolly Roger taught the dock dogs was to run the wrong way up a one-way street when the dog catcher was after them in his truck.

Sometimes Jolly Roger would let himself be caught so the others could get away. Jolly Roger had been caught lots of times. There would always be someone watching who would go and tell The Kid. The Kid would go to the dog pound and pay a fine, and get Jolly Roger out. A number of times The Kid was not needed. Jolly Roger had broken away from the dog catcher 7 times, had broken out of the dog catcher's truck 9 times, and had broken out of the dog pound 5 times—a total of 21 escapes.

Even though The Kid didn't see Jolly Roger every day, Jolly Roger was still his dog. Jolly Roger was not The Kid's dog because The Kid took Jolly Roger home with him, and he was not The Kid's dog

because The Kid fed him—because The Kid didn't do those things very often once Jolly Roger was king of the waterfront. He was not even The Kid's dog because The Kid would go down to the dog pound to pay Jolly Roger's fine when he got caught. Jolly Roger was The Kid's dog because The Kid was the only person Jolly Roger would allow to pet him, and The Kid was the only person who could get Jolly Roger to play, and The Kid was the only person who could get Jolly Roger to lie on his back and wave all four paws in the air.

VI

While Jolly Roger was clearly The Kid's dog and nobody else's, he also had a great many friends, human and animal. At times, Jolly Roger would disappear from the waterfront. People would report seeing him a mile away at the other end of Hoboken, or two or three miles away in the next town.

"I saw Jolly Roger way up in Weehawken," someone might say.

"Jolly Roger was having a hamburger over in Jersey City this morning," someone else might say.

Every afternoon, during his break, the cook from the Five Star Chinese-American Restaurant would appear at the iron fence, carrying two big plates of shrimp egg foo yung, Jolly Roger's favorite.

The cops especially liked Jolly Roger, and nearly every time the dog catcher got him, they would arrest the dog catcher and throw him in jail for a few hours.

And there was a millionaire who parked his car at the garage five days a week. Sometimes, on a Friday, the millionaire would invite Jolly Roger to get into his car, which was a big and fancy one. Jolly Roger would hop in, and sit on the front seat. The millionaire would take Jolly Roger to his estate in the country, and entertain him for the weekend. When Jolly Roger would come back on Monday, he would burp a good deal, and hardly touch his egg foo yung.

VII

Once there was a big storm with high winds. Jolly Roger was sitting on the end of the pier, where the Erie Lakawanna tugboats tie up, looking into the distance and thinking. A really powerful gust of wind lifted Jolly Roger right off the pier and into the river ten feet below.

The river was whipped by the wind, and the current was strong. Jolly Roger was carried out into the channel, where he was certainly drowned. Peo-

ple saw this happen, but there was no chance of saving Jolly Roger. It all happened too fast. They told The Kid, who felt very bad. Everyone on the waterfront felt bad. They hated to think that they would never see Jolly Roger again.

Three days later, Jolly Roger crawled out of a storm sewer which connected with the river. He was very tired, and soaking wet. He slept all day at the garage. The Kid brought him bowls of hot soup whenever he woke up. The next morning he went back to the docks.

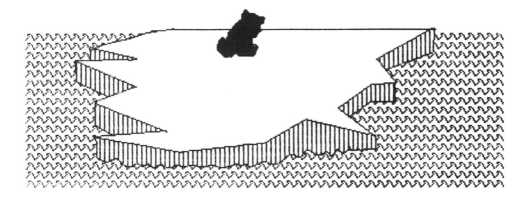

Once, in the middle of winter, Jolly Roger was sitting on the frozen edge of the river, when the piece of ice he was sitting on broke off. Jolly Roger, still sitting calmly, floated out into the middle of the river and began moving into New York Harbor. He was in mid-river, heading for the Statue of Liberty when he was sighted by the crew of one of the Erie Lakawanna tugs. They called to him, and he hopped off the ice, swam to the tug, was taken aboard, and brought back to Hoboken wrapped in a towel. Jolly Roger had five sardine sandwiches prepared by the cook on the tug boat. He appeared to have enjoyed the experience.

VIII

Some men came to see Marvin the Ape.

"We thought we would tear down your garage, and build a Turkish bath," the men said. "Of course, if you don't want to sell it to us, we could tap lumps on your head for two or three hours while you think it over."

"As a matter of fact," Marvin the Ape said, "I

have been thinking about getting into the potato chip business down in Florida."

"Fine," the men said. "Here's the money. Get lost."

"Kid, you want to go to Florida and get rich in the potato chip game?" Marvin the Ape asked The Kid.

"I guess so," The Kid said. The Kid was thinking about how hard it would be to leave Jolly Roger.

"Get your stuff together, bean-head," Marvin the Ape said. "We'll leave for Florida tomorrow."

The Kid wandered out into the alley. He was thinking about his dog, Jolly Roger, the king of the waterfront. Jolly Roger had been king of the waterfront for a long time—longer than any other dog had ever been. Sooner or later, Jolly Roger would have to retire—but then he would probably go to live with his millionaire friend in the country, or retire to a warm corner of the Five Star Chinese-American Restaurant. He wouldn't want to go to Florida with The Kid and Marvin the Ape to be in the potato chip business.

Just then, Jolly Roger himself turned up. The Kid noticed that Jolly Roger had gotten sort of gray around the muzzle. Jolly Roger wagged his tail, and

made a few playful jumps of the sort he never let anyone see but The Kid.

The Kid scratched Jolly Roger's head and told him all about how he had to go to Florida to be in the potato chip business. He told Jolly Roger how much he'd miss him. He told him goodbye.

The next morning, The Kid loaded his stuff into Marvin the Ape's big, shiny car. They were going to drive straight through to Florida, non-stop. The Kid took a last look at Hoboken before getting into the car. Marvin the Ape started the engine. The Kid shut the door. The car started rolling.

Just then The Kid and Marvin the Ape heard furious barking. It was Jolly Roger running at top speed after the car. Marvin the Ape stopped the car. The Kid opened the door. Jolly Roger jumped into the car, and settled down on the front seat between The Kid and Marvin the Ape.

"Jolly! Do you want to come to Florida with us, and be in the potato chip business?" The Kid asked.

"Woof woof woof woof!" Jolly Roger barked.

"You're going to retire from being king of the waterfront?"

"Woof woof woof woof!" Jolly Roger said.

"I guess he's coming with us," The Kid said.

"I guess so," Marvin the Ape said. He stepped on the gas, and the big car started moving toward the Jersey Turnpike.

40